AMAZING RHYMES

AMAZING RHYMES

PRAGYA BHAGWAT

Kalamos Literary Services LLP

Kalamos Literary Services LLP
Email: info@kalamos.co.in | editorial@kalamos.co.in
First Published in 2018
by
Kalamos Literary Services
ISBN- 978-93-87780-12-5

Amazing Rhymes
Pragya Bhagwat

Cover designed and typeset in Kalamos Literary Services LLP

~FOREWORD~

MANISH SISODIA
मनीष सिसोदिया

DEPUTY CHIEF MINISTER
GOVT. OF NCT OF DELHI
उप मुख्यमंत्री, दिल्ली सरकार
DELHI SECTT, I.P. ESTATE,
दिल्ली सचिवालय, आई॰पी॰एस्टेट,
NEW DELHI-110002
नई दिल्ली-110002
Email. msisodia.delhi@gov.in
D.O. No : DYCM/2018/652
Date : 14 अगस्त, 2018

शुभकामना संदेश

आठ वर्षीय प्रज्ञा द्वारा लिखी गई यह किताब किसी उत्कृष्ट कृति से कम नहीं है। वह अपनी कविताओं में मौसम, रंग और अन्य कई रोजमर्रा की चीजों के बारे में बात करती है और वह उसमें ये भी प्रयास करती हैं कि हर शब्द को एक नया अर्थ दे पाए। इस बाल अवस्था में लेखन की गुणवत्ता प्रशंसनीय है। मुझे पूर्ण विश्वास है कि समय के साथ लेखन की कला में और अधिक उत्कृष्टता का समावेश होगा।

मैं प्रज्ञा की कार्य प्रगति और उनकी सोच प्रक्रिया की सराहना करता हूं और उम्मीद करता हूं कि वह अपनी कविताओं के माध्यम से कई और बच्चों को प्रेरित करेगी। यह किताब प्रत्येक बच्चे को पढ़नी चाहिए। मैं प्रज्ञा के उज्ज्वल भविष्य की कामना करता हूं।

(मनीष सिसोदिया)

~PRAISE FOR THE BOOK~

Imaginative and full of joy, Pragya's rhymes take us into her beautiful world as we get a peep into a child's creative mind.
- **Rushati Ghosh, Author of The Turbo Gang**

~*~

Pragya is a free bird. Who explore the world of creativity. Her poetry is magical n musical. Just feel it n it does wonders...
- **Ms. Seema Ahuja, Learning officer, Little millennium Education Pvt. LTD.**

~*~

Beautifully narrated and illustrated, 'Amazing Rhymes' is a collection of poems that every child would cherish.

Dr. Mrs Vimal Rarh
Joint director,
Guru Angad Dev Teaching Learning Centre of MHRD,
Govt. of India

~*~

Lancer's is proud of you!
"Poetry is when an emotion has found thought and thought has found words ".
Kudos to Pragya, a budding poet whose aesthetic senses have painted this earthern world in colorful hues. Your poems are a profound expression of what's inside you. Your kaleidoscope of poem focuses on everything and anything there is, making your poems as diverse as life itself.
We feel, the arrival of a new poet doesn't cause stars to wobble or birds to fall from trees but heads to turn you are going to liven up this world with your kinetic enthusiasm
Lancer's wish you the hall of fame in all your endeavors.
- **Lancers Convent, Prashant Vihar**

INDEX

1

ICE CREAM ICE CREAM

Ice cream ice cream I had a **dream**
Yesterday night I had this **dream**
About **ice cream ice cream** in my **dream**
I saw a **dream** of so many flavors and so many colors
My mouth was watering as a **cream**
Oh, what a treat it was in my **ice cream dream**

2
WATER

Water water is our life
Water water we can't survive
Water is all around
Without it, neither me nor is a life

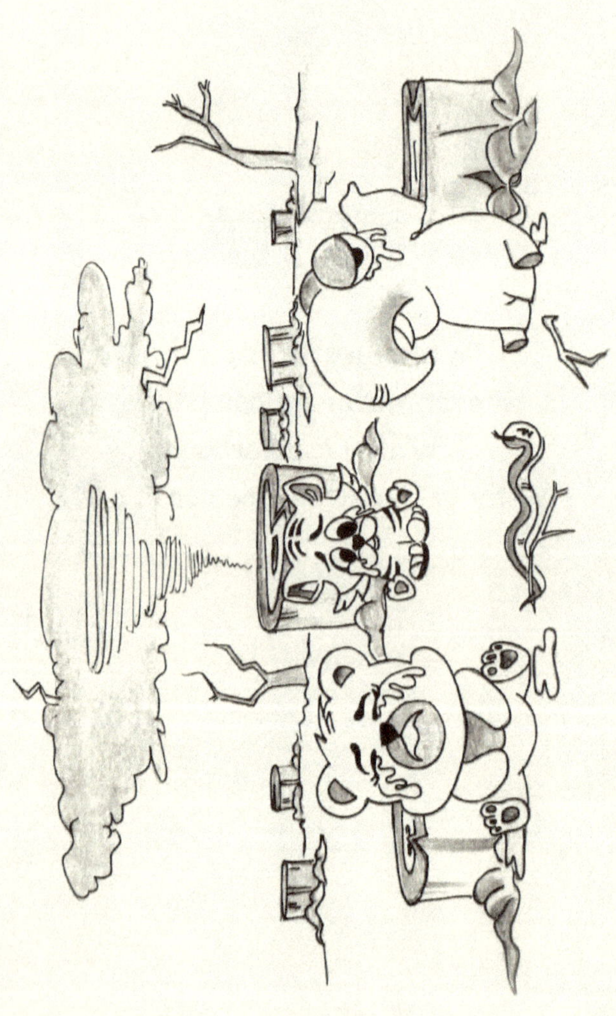

3
TREES

Trees are our life
Trees are our world
So stop cutting them
Else we will not survive
Without oxygen how would you survive?
The animals won't have any home, neither would I
The sky will be completely dark with no clean air
Around the sky
Stop destroying the only planet
And our life
Stop cutting trees
Else we will not survive

4
BOOK

When the world is dark for me
A good book helps me shine my world up
A book is a person's best friend
It tells about itself,
And the world

5
CAMPING TOGETHER

Let's go camping together
In the breeze of the trees
In the shade of the trees, we read a book
Let's go camping together
Hike all day
Search all day
No responsibility
And just be free
Let's go camping together
In the breeze of the trees

6
SILVER LIGHT

Moonlight in the sky
As a silver brightness that shines the sky
That lights up the night
Not as bright as day
But a silver light in the sky

7
WEATHER

There are many kinds of weather into play
Like fall as leaves and winter as cold
Summer so hot and spring so green
So the weather tell you
What time of year it is and
What to wear or play
Weather, weather, weather, let's play together

8
FALL SEASON

Oh dear tree, it's the time of year for your leaves to
fall
In a colorful manner
So, we can play
In your color of fall
Let's jump and play in the puddle of leaves
Cause it's fall, fall, fall, yay!!!!!

9
SPRING

The earth looks wonderful wearing a green gown
With its lovely sound humming around
The birds fly by
In the lovely sky
And bees fluttering by
The breeze fills the sky with joy
I wish spring lasts
Forever
But other seasons
Are waiting to come
But we know
Spring you're coming again
With your lovely colors here and there

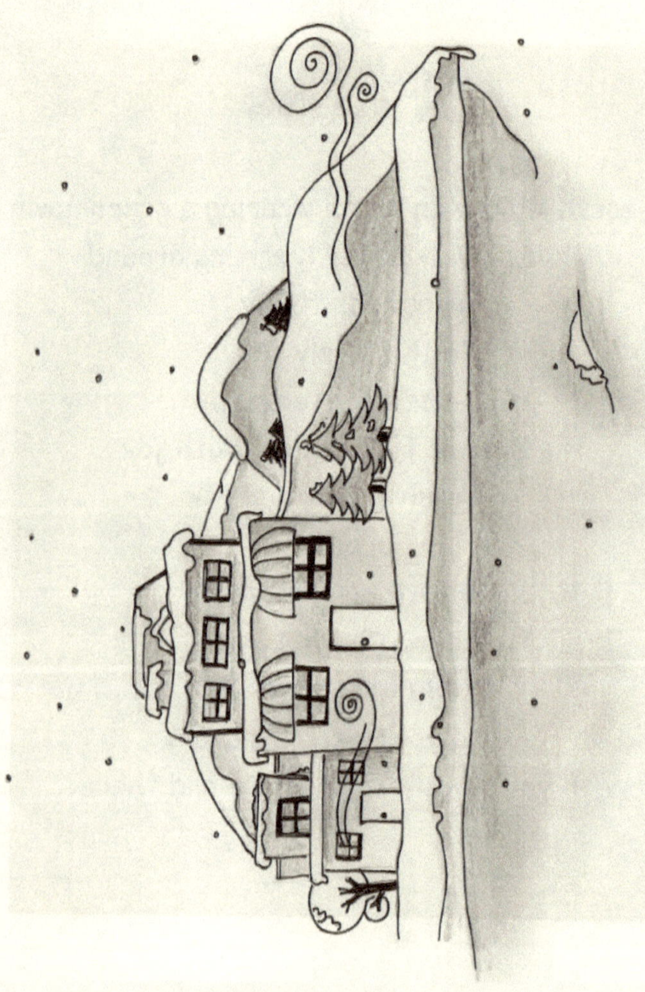

10
WINTER

The wind is blowing hard in the time
Everyone stops and goes inside
In winters everything
Looks like a frosted cake

11
SUMMER

Sun, sun, sun, it's summer-time for you to play
The season of the sun is here
Let your son and hare
Go out to play
In the hay
Hey let's play, play, play

12
CHRISTMAS

Christmas, Christmas the jolly laughs are here
Ho, ho, ho, so Santa wants to say
Down the chimney when you are fast asleep
Presents will be at the bottom of your Christmas tree

ROBOT

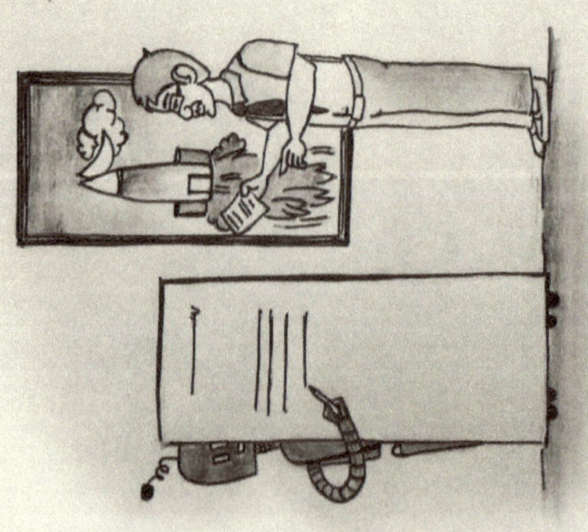

13
POWER OF IMAGINATION

Imagine the world around yourself
Imagine the world as a change
Imagination can build what hasn't ever been invented
Or thought of

GOT IT!

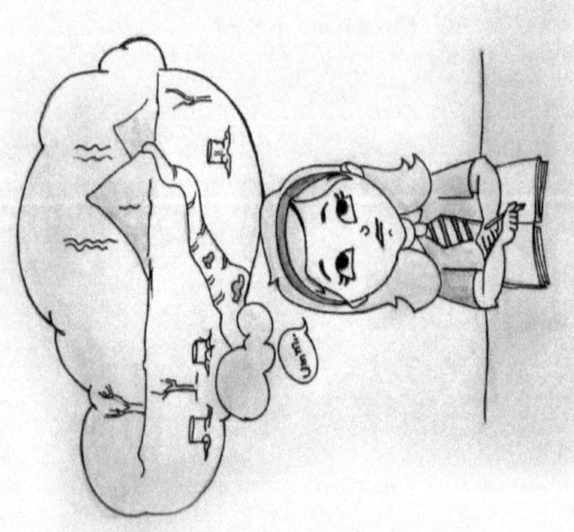
Umm...

14
OBSERVE

Observe the world as a change
And everything can be clear
So open your heart and observe
If you do that you will get all
The answers you need

15
SIMPLE MACHINE

They might be simple but very useful
There are six of them, all waiting for a user to use
All say let us do your work and make your day
Let me introduce you to all of them
Pulleys, they help you pick up things
Wedges and lever help us cut the things
Screws help us hold the things tight
Now you know who I am
I am a simple machine
I am here to help you do things

16
CHRISTMAS DISHES

Christmas dishes for Santa
As he comes to your home
Like candy canes and Christmas cake
Because he needs a snack
Traveling all the way from the winter zap

AAAAAAAA

17
FANS

Fans are old
Fans are new
They give air
Because that's what they have to do
With blades or not
It is a fan
They make you cool and fresh

18
TOY IMAGINATION

Well I wonder about the toys I have
Dolls as real girls
And teddies roaming wild
Figures as little dwarves
I wish they were real
As it would be fun to play

19
SUMMER

In summer we go to the beach
And play in the sea
But don't forget
To put sunscreen

20
DOGS

Dogs so sweet, dogs so cute
As sugar or sweet
Or even you
Dogs so sweet, dogs so cute
But they even pee on your t-shirt or stool

21
IMAGINATION OF BOOKS

Fairy tales adventures and many other things
Are kept inside a book, that is what I think
Fairies and castles
We might even meet a king
Which come together in a small thing
So whenever you are bored
Just take a book because
That is what I think

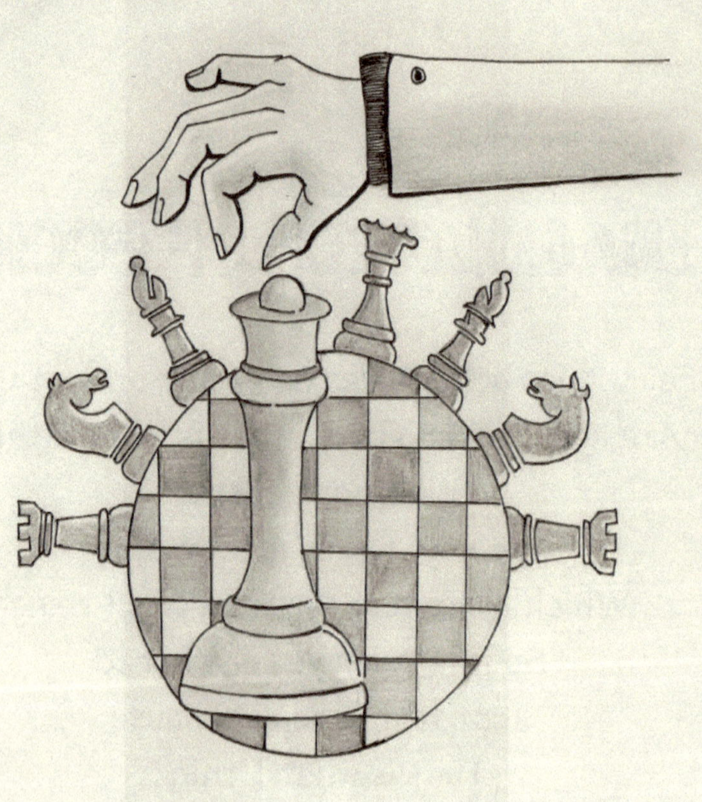

22
CHESS

Chess is fun, chess is great
It makes your mind really great
It has many pieces
So that you can play

23
IMAGINATION

Imagination is that is in all
It allows you to create and learn
And build that you can
Open your heart and imagine as big as you can

School Bus
Poem Recitation
English Test Result
Test...
SCHOOL

24
GOING TO SCHOOL

Going to school might look easy to you
But at many places
There are difficulties
That get in their way
But still, they go to school in any case

PINK
PURPLE
RED
GREEN
BLUE

25
COLORS

Colors are fun
Colors are great
You can play with them at any place
Pink or purple it doesn't matter
They all are the same in any case

26
MY SISTER IS COMING

My sister is coming this afternoon
Oh I am so excited I don't know what to do
My mother is in trouble cleaning the house
But I am still excited because
My sister's coming this afternoon!!!

27
DOLLS

Such cute faces to play with
Oh, it is so much fun
With colorful clothes, they are no. 1
Dolls are fun and so very cute
Oh I never want to stop playing with you

28
CURIOSITY

Curiosity is in the air
That
Flows through the
Mind
And then to the nerves that
Rise

29
CLOCKS

Tick – tock the alarm clock says
Time to wake up from your bed
Tick tock tick tock the alarm clock says
Time to eat breakfast that's what it says
Tick tock tick tock the alarm clock says
It is time to eat brunch that's what it says
Tick tock tick tock the alarm clock says
Time to nap that's what it says
Tick tock tick tock the alarm clock says
Time to play that's what it says
Tick tock tick tock the alarm clock says
It time to study that's what it says
Tick tock tick tock the alarm clock says
Time eat dinner that's what it says
Tick tock tick tock the alarm clock says
Time to sleep that's what it says
Tick tock tick tock
Let's repeat all again

2½
8⁶
4√64
5X12
3+5
+269

30
MATHS

Oh! Maths is so **tricky**
But sometimes it's so **easy**
It makes my head go **dizzy**
It has so many operations
To give us a solution
Addition and multiplication give you
Larger numbers
Subtraction and division give you
Smaller numbers
But they all have a connection
To give you a solution

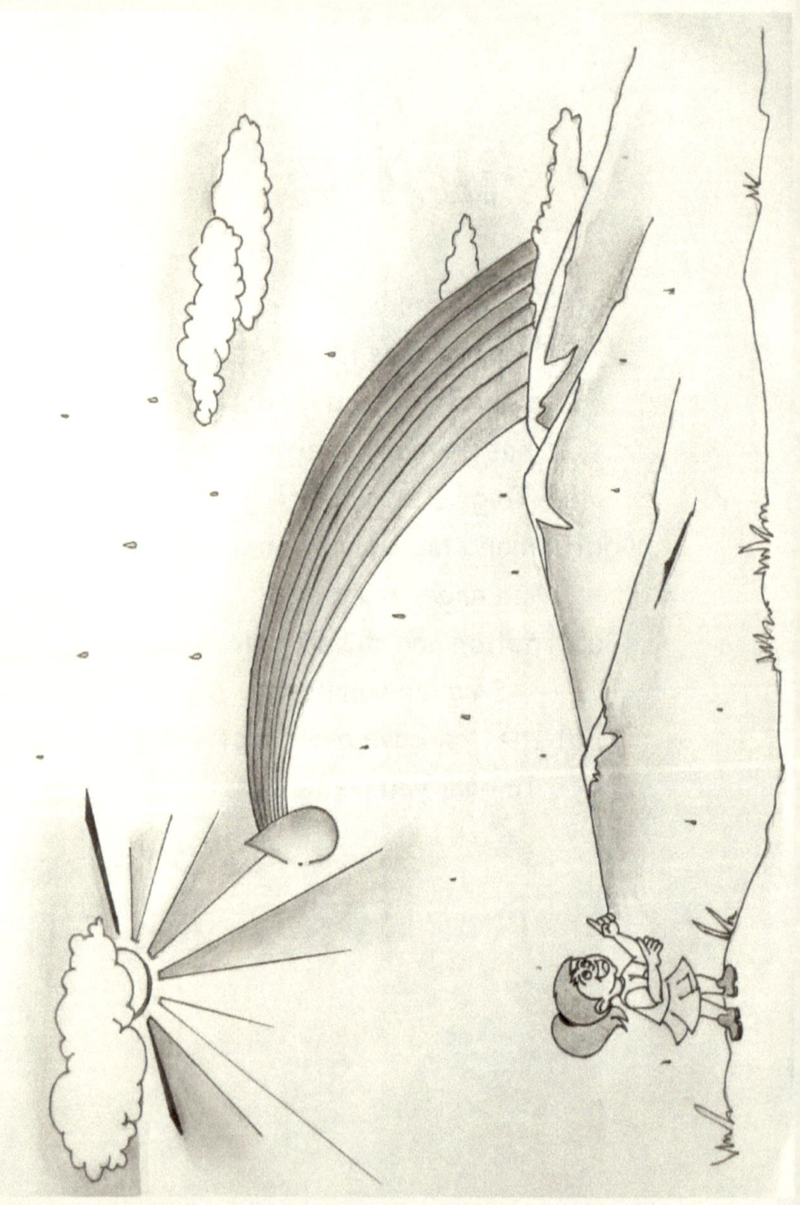

31
RAINBOW

The formula of a rainbow
Is light and water
That split up in 7 colors
So you can smile
But it goes away
When the clouds run away
But do visit again
With its lovely color once again

32
FRIENDS

Friends will help you
They'll always stay by your side
Whether you are playing,
Dancing or singing or even when nobody is with you
Friends will always be there with you
Friends are special and very important
And be with you for a lifetime

33
SPRING

The season of new life is here
Leaves and flowers bloom everywhere
The wind
Is blowing here and there
The season of colors is here
Now let's play
In the color
All along

34
INQUISITIVE

Observers and thinkers are inquisitive
Ask many questions and think
Think about it some more
Be inquisitive
And every problem can be solved
So think, think, and think
And be inquisitive

About Pragya Bhagwat

Pragya Bhagwat has been a very inquisitive and innovative child since her infancy days. She was passionate about books and has been listening to rhymes since her toddler days. She likes to explore the world and beyond through her eyes and wants to become an astronomer when she grows up.

She has immense capability to grasp and reciprocate anything that she sees or listens. She has the ability to create rhymes/poems out of anything. And now when she has collated few of her best collection, she is ready to publish her first set of rhymes for the world.

ACKNOWLEDGEMENTS

A big thank you…

To my parents who have always inspired me and supported in whatever I wanted to do. They have been a true inspiration and always set a new benchmark for me to excel. It is their efforts that I could identify my true capability and was able to come out with my first book of rhymes. My parents knew what was right for me during my early childhood and their guidance and upbringing helped me become what I am today.

To my school teachers, right from kindergarten till now. They have been very supportive and always encouraged me to come forward with my inquisitive and always challenging questions and reasonings. It is their effort that I can explore relentlessly and think beyond convention.

To my creative publisher Anuj Bhaiya, who gave me this opportunity to outshine and help publish my first book of rhymes. To my Illustrator, who understood my imagination and was able to put life to my rhymes through the graphics.

To all my grandparents, their blessings are always with me and will keep me strong and growing forever.